This is a story about Harquin the Fox. He lived with his family. Their home was at the top of a hill, and they were able to live peacefully because the local squire and his gamekeeper, who used to hunt foxes, did not know they were there.

HARQUIN

the fox who went down to the valley

JOH AM

RED FOX

for Lucy

A Red Fox Book

Published by Random Century Children's Books
20 Vauxhall Bridge Road, London SW1V 2SA
A division of the Random Century Group

London Melbourne Sydney Auckland
Johannesburg and agencies throughout the world

First published by Jonathan Cape Limited 1967
Red Fox edition 1991

Made and printed in Hong Kong

ISBN 0 09 9825 104

Now Harquin's parents would often warn the young foxes. 'You can play here on the hill,' they would say, 'but don't go down to the valley, otherwise the huntsmen will see you and follow you back here and we will no longer be safe.'

But Harquin was bored with playing on top of the hill.

He would secretly go down to the valley at night while everyone was asleep. There were many interesting things. Harquin liked to smell the flowers that grew in the gardens.

In the valley there were also some very treacherous marshes which nobody dared to cross for fear of sinking in the mud. But Harquin discovered a secret route across them, and on the other side he used to catch rabbits and chickens.

One evening Harquin's father called all the family together. 'I have reason to believe', he said, 'that one of you has been going out at night. Now I must warn you all again about going down to the valley. Remember what happened to your uncle,' he added, pointing to the picture on the wall. 'He was caught by the huntsmen.'

But Harquin would not listen. He used to run through the village, making sure that he was not seen.

One night when Harquin was returning home, he *was* seen by the gamekeeper.

Bang! Bang! went the gamekeeper's gun. The shot missed Harquin but gave him a terrible fright.

'I didn't know there were foxes living around here,' thought the gamekeeper. 'I must tell the squire about this so that he can bring the hunt here.'

Harquin's parents heard the bangs and saw Harquin rushing home. 'I warned you,' said his father. 'Now we'll all be killed when the huntsmen find us.'

'Whatever shall we do?' cried his mother.

The next day the gamekeeper went to see the squire and told him about the fox. 'Good!' said the squire. 'We'll take the hunt there on Sunday. We've never been up the valley before: I didn't know there were foxes there.'

Harquin's parents feared the next hunt would come looking for them. 'It's best that we remain here and just hope that they won't discover our home,' the parents told the little foxes.

But Harquin was making his own plans. 'I must lead the hunt away from here,' he thought.

Early on Sunday morning Harquin left and went down to the valley. He hid in some undergrowth where he was able to watch the huntsmen gathering in the village square. As soon as the master blew his horn and the hunt began to move off, Harquin rushed ahead and waited.

He waited until he was quite sure the huntsmen had seen him.

‘We’re not far behind him now,’
shouted the squire.

Harquin ran for his life. 'If only I can reach the marshes in time!' he thought.

At last he reached the edge of the marsh and sped along his secret path.

But the hounds, horses and huntsmen did not know the way across and...

SPLOSH! SPLASH!
they all fell into the slimy mud.

The squire, who had been thrown into the marsh head-first, was furious and shook with anger. ‘Call off the hounds,’ he bellowed. ‘We cannot hunt in this bog. The hounds can’t find the scent and we shall lose them.’

The squire was so angry that he broke his riding crop. ‘Where’s that gamekeeper fellow who suggested this hunt?’ he roared.

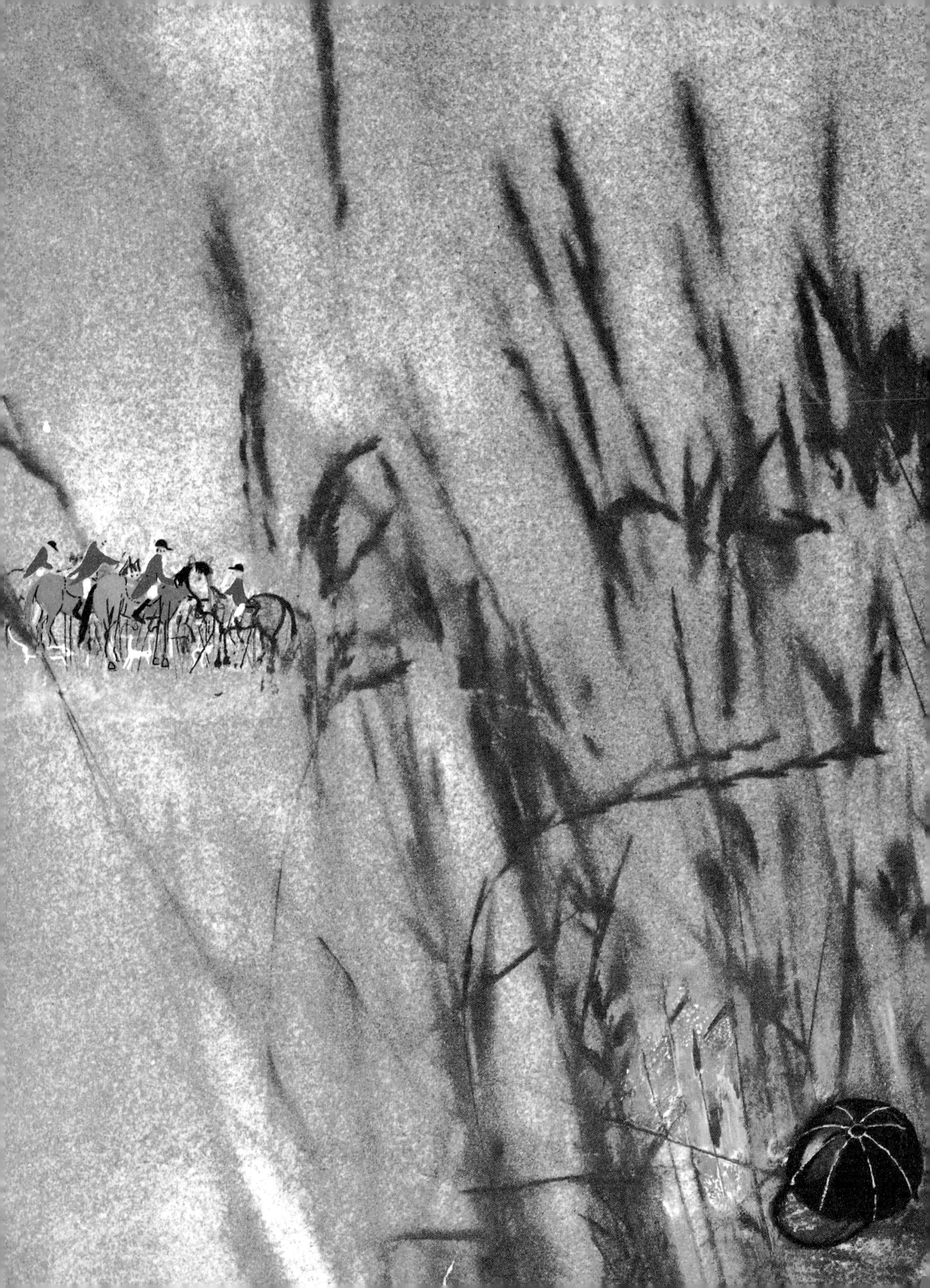

93
e Endotracheal intubation
180, *180*, **193**
ening in *see* Tracheostomies
122, 181
ood, 79, 80–81, **123**
nergy requirement, 84
is, 257
a, **268**
, 255, *256*
gs/oocysts, *240*
mnali, 257
, 85
0–92, *90, 91*
f tubes, 92
6–88
geal, 86–88, *87, 88*, 293
y, 88–90, *89*
ues, 267–276
nd subcutaneous, **268**
t aid, **193**
273–276, *273*
330–332
340–343, *341*
adiographs, 209–210

172, *173*
stic, 202, 227–228
s/oocysts, *240*
177
n, 47, 48
–220
7, 43–47, *44, 69*
rgencies, **122**
itoring, **117**
tients, 58
nary catheters
–49
s, 62–63
, 61
–261
itoring, 48

  incontinence of, 56, 57, 58
  manual expression of bladder, 47–48
  normal volume, **26**
  output measurement, **26**, 37, 48, 59, 62, 79, 95, 97, **117**
  peritoneal dialysis, 49–50
  renal patients, 59
  samples, 258–259
  scalds, 57
  sediment, 259, 260–261, *261*
  smell, 259
  specific gravity, 63, 259–260
  urination during fluid therapy, 75
  urination post-anaesthesia, 120
  water balance in the body, 66, 74
Urogenital system
  dystocia, 192–199, **197**, 198*b*, **198**
  injuries, **193**
  radiography, 218–221
  see also Sexing
Urography, intravenous, 218–219, *218*
Uterus
  parturition, **197**, **198**
  prolapse, **193**

V

Vacutainers, 356–357, *356*, **356**
Vaginal speculums, 45–46
Vaginourethrography, 219–220
Vaporizers, anaesthetic machines, *100*, 101, **102**
Vasculogenic shock, **192**
Veins, 'raising', 11
  see also Intravenous *entries; specific veins*
Velpeau sling, **158**, 159–161, *162*
Venables plate, **170**
Ventral, meaning, *205*
Ventricular arrhythmias/fibrillation, **122**
Vernier scale, 235–236, *235*
Veterinary Surgeons Act (1966), 175, 263–264
Viruses, ELISA tests, 230
Volumetric pipettes, 236
Volvulus, **193**
Vomiting
  inducing, **184**, 189, **189**
  rabbits, **297**
Vomiting patients, 55–56, 60, 67, 74

W

Walking
  diabetes mellitus patients, 62
  supported, 51, *51*, 57
Washing soda crystals, **189**
Wasp stings, **191**
Waste, disposal of laboratory, 237
Water
  autoclaves, 128–129, 231
  oral fluid therapy, 68
  pre-anaesthetic, 101–103
Water baths, 237
Water, body
  balance, 66–67
  content, 66–81
  deficit replacement fluids, 67
  loss calculations, 74
Water deprivation test, 62, 63
Weaning age
  ferrets, **310**
  rabbits, **290**
  small rodents, **290**
Wedding rings, 132
Weedkiller poisoning, **184**
Weight, body *see* Bodyweight
Wet-to-dry dressings, 156, **157**
White blood cells, *243*
  counting fluids, **247**
  differential count, 250, 251–252, *251*
  total count, 244–246, **246**, *247*
Whole blood, 67, 68
Wing clipping, 317
Wood's lamp, detecting *Microsporum canis*, 255–256
Worm eggs/oocysts, *240*
  counting, 239–240, *239*
Wounds
  bandaging, 157–165, **158**, **178**, 348–352
  classification, **154**
  closure, 271–273, *272*, 274
  debridement, 272
  drainage, 167–168
  dressings, 156, 157, **157**, 176
  emergency first aid *see* First aid
  horses, 348–352
  management, 153–159, 176, **178**, 190–192
  preventing contamination of *see* Asepsis in theatre practice
  suturing, 169–170, *171*, **172**, 272, 282–283

X

X-rays, diagnostic *see* Radiography
Xylazine, **189**

Z

Zoonotic diseases, 42, 52–53, 55, 58
  parasitology, 255
  reptiles, 322–323, 325

P

Packed cell volume (PCV), 74, 242–244, *245*, **246**
Packing materials for sterilization, 130–132, **131**
Pain
  local anaesthesia, 121
  pancreatitis, 60
  post-anaesthesia, 120
    ferrets, 315
    rabbits, 299
    small rodents, 310
  pre-anaesthetic assessment, 104
  premedicant drugs, **105**
Palmar, meaning, *205*
'Palming', 264, *264*
Palpebral reflex, **117**, 298, 331
Pancreatic disease, 60–62
Paper drapes, **131**
Papilloma, **268**
Paracetamol poisoning, **184**
Paraplegic patients, 56–57
  supported exercise, 51, *51*, 57
Paraquat poisoning, **184**
Parasitology, 255–258
  ectoparasites, 256–258, *257*
  Giemsa stain for blood parasites, 249–250
  ringworm, 255–256
  worm egg counting, 239–240
Parenteral feeding, 83, 95–97
  feeding regimes, 95–97
  food choice, 96–97
  jugular vein, 95–97
  monitoring, 97
  nutrition calculations, 95–97
Parturition, 192–199, **197**, 198*b*, **198**
Passive physiotherapy, 50–52, 57
Pedal reflex, **117**
  rabbits, 298
Pedicle grafts, **154**
Pelvis, radiography, 207–209, *208*
Penile injuries, **193**
Penrose drains, 167–168, *168*
Perineal injuries, **193**
Perineural anaesthesia, **124**
Periodontal disease, 172, **173**, **174**
Periodontitis, **173**
Peripheral circulation, physiotherapy, 50, 51–52
Peripheral oedema, 77
Peripheral pulses, **117**
Peritoneal dialysis, 49–50
Pethidine, **105**
Petroleum gauze, **157**
Petroleum product poisoning, **184**
Pharyngostomy tube feeding, 88–90, *89*
Pharynx, 108, *108*
  anaesthetic emergencies, **122**
  emergency first aid, **193**
  foreign body obstruction, 180, **193**
Phenol poisoning, **184**
Phenothiazine, **105**
Phenylbutazone poisoning, **184**
Phosphorus, renal patients, 59
Physiotherapy, passive, 50–52, 57
Pigeon bait poisoning, **184**
Pinna
  suturing wounds to, 282–283
  treating aural haematomata, 283–284, *283*
Pipettes, 236
Pituitary gland, 62
Plantar, meaning, *205*
Plaque, **173**
Plasma, 67, 68
Plasma volume, 67, 72, 74
Plasma water, *66*
Plaster of Paris casts, **158**, 165
Platelets (thrombocytes), *243*, **246**
Plates, bone, **170**
Pneumocystography, 220–221
Pneumonia, hypostatic, 50–51, 57
Pneumothorax, **193**
Poisoning
  convulsions, 57
  emergency first aid, 183–190, **184**, **189**
  hepatic disease, 59
  vomiting due to, 55, **184**
Polishing, teeth, 170–173
Pollution control, anaesthetic gases, 115
Polydioxanone sutures, **172**
Polyglactin 910 sutures, **172**
Polyglycolic acid sutures, **172**
Polyps, **193**
Polythene bags, sterilization packing, **131**
Polyuria, 62
Post, sending samples by, 252
Potassium, cardiac failure, 58
Pouches, sterilization packing, **131**
Poultices, **157**
Premedicants, 104, **105**, 314
Pressage bandages, horses, 350–351
Pressure, haemorrhage control, **178**
Pressure gauges, 100, *100*, *101*, **102**
Prolapse
  eye, **193**
  rectum, **193**
  uterus, **193**
Propofol, **106**, **297**, **330**
Protein
  hepatic patients, 59–60
  renal patients, 59
Proximal, meaning, *205*
Puberty, age at
  ferrets, **310**
  rabbits, **290**
  small rodents, **290**
Pulse
  anaesthesia monitoring, **117**
  fluid therapy monitoring, 77
  horses, 345–346
  measuring, 27, 28–29, 42, 345–346
  normal parameters, **26**
    ferrets, **310**
    horses, **345**
    rabbits, **290**
    small rodents, **290**
  pre-anaesthetic check, 104
  signs of shock, **192**
Pulse oximetry, 31–32, *32*, *36*, **117**
Punch biopsies, 269, *269*
Puncture wounds, **154**

Q

QBC Autoread (IDEXX), 230

R

Rabbit, 289–299
  biological data, **290**
  blood sampling, **308**
  drug administration, 291–296
  general anaesthesia, 296–299
  handling and restraint, 289, *291*
  pedal reflexes, **117**
  sexing, 289–291, *292*
Radiation, sterilization by, 128, 129
Radiography, 202–228
  contrast media, 215–222
  equipment maintenance, 226–227
  patient positioning, 203–215
  patient preparation, 203
  processing techniques, 222–225
  X-ray machine maintenance, 226–227
  X-ray machine setting up, 202–203
  X-ray room preparation, 203
Rat, **290**, **297**, 304–306, **307**, **308**
Rat bait poisoning, **184**
Rattus norvegicus *see* Rat
Records *see* Charts
Recovery position, *182*
Rectal injuries, **193**
Recumbent patients, 56–57
  catheterization *see* Urinary catheters
  passive physiotherapy, 50–52
Red blood cells, *243*
  counting fluids, **247**
  normal ranges, **246**

Red blood cells (*Continued*)
  replacement, 67, 68
  reticulocyte count, 248–249
  total count, 246–248, *246*, *247*
Reflexes, anaesthesia monitoring, **117**, 298, 322, 331
Refractometers, 259–260, *259*
Regional anaesthesia, **124**
Renal disease, 58–59
  convulsions, 57
  diabetes insipidus, 62
  peritoneal dialysis, 49–50
  uraemia, **193**
Renal function, anaesthesia monitoring, **117**
Reptiles, 322–332
  chelonians, 325–328
  lizards, 328–329, *330*
  snakes, **191**, 323–325
  zoonoses, 322–323, 325
Respiration
  anaesthesia monitoring, **117**, **119**, 298
  anaesthetic emergencies, 121, **122**, **123**
  anaesthetic gas flow rate, 115–116
  anaesthetic induction agents, **106**
  artificial, 181–182, 183
  asphyxia, **177**, 180
  epileptic patient monitoring, 57
  first aid, 176, **177**, 180, 181–183, **193**
  fluid therapy monitoring, 77
  horses, 346–347
  measuring rate of, 29–30, 42, 346–347
  normal parameters, **26**
    ferrets, **310**
    horses, **345**
    rabbits, **290**
    small rodents, **290**
  pre-anaesthetic check, 104
Restraint of patients *see* Handling and restraint
Resuscitation, mouth-to-nose, 182–183
Reticulocyte count, 248–249, *249*
Ring bandages, **158**, *166*
Ringer's solution, 67
Rings, 132
Ringworm
  culture for, 255
  microscopic appearance, *256*
  Wood's lamp to detect *Microsporum canis*, 255–256
Robert Jones bandage, **158**, 159–165, *160*, 351, **351**
Rodenticide poisoning, **184**
Rodents, small, 299–310
  biological data, **290**
  bites from, 299
  chinchilla, **290**, 299–300, **307**, **308**
  drug administration, 305–308
  general anaesthesia, **297**, 308–310
  gerbil, **290**, 300, **307**, **308**
  guinea pig, **290**, **297**, 300–302, **307**, **308**
  hamster, **290**, *300*, 302–303, **307**, **308**
  mouse, **290**, **297**, *300*, 303–304, **307**, **308**
  rat, **290**, **297**, 304–305, **307**, **308**
Romanowsky stains, 250, 251
Rotameters (flowmeters), 100, *100*, *101*, **102**
Royal College of Veterinary Surgeons, 263–264
Rubber endotracheal tubes, 108, 110
Rupture wounds, **154**
Rush pins, **170**

S

Safety guidelines
  horse handling, 334
  laboratory tests, 230–261
Salbutamol poisoning, **184**
Saline, 61, 67, 68, 69, 74
  flushing abscess wounds, 267, *267*
  formol, 252
  heparinized, 72
Salmonella, 322, 325
Salt, cardiac failure patients, 58
Saphenous vein
  fluid therapy, 72–73, 276
  injections
    cats, 21
    dogs, 11–12, *12*
    small rodents, **307**
Sarcoma, soft-tissue, **268**
Sarcoptes, 256–258, *257*
Scalds
  first aid, 179
  urine, 57
Scaling, teeth, 170–173
Scalpels, 264–266, *265*
Scavenging (by patients), 55
Scavenging (pollution control), 115
Schiotz tonometers, 38–39
Schirmer strips, 37–38, *38*
Scissors, 265–266, *265*
Scratches, avoiding
  cats, 14, 15
  rabbits, 289
Screws, bone, **170**
Scrub, surgical, 134–135, *135*
Scrub nurses, 145, 146
Scrub suits, **137**
Seabird bait poisoning, **184**
Sebaceous adenocarcinoma, **268**
Sebaceous adenoma, **268**
Sedation, 104, **105**, **297**
Sediment, urine, 259, 260–261, *261*
Seizures *see* Epilepsy
Seldinger jugular catheter placement, 276–278, *276*, *277*
Self-seal pouches, sterilization packing, **131**
Sensible water loss, 66, 74
Sepsis, illness energy requirement, 84
Seton drains, **167**
Sevoflurane, **107**, **321**, **330**
Sexing
  ferrets, 311–312
  rabbits, 289–291, *292*
  small rodents, 299–300, *300*, 301–302, *302*, 303–304, 305
Sharps, disposal, 237
Shearing wounds, **154**
Sherman plate, **170**
Shock, 190–192, **192**
Shoulder
  injuries, **158**
  radiographs, 211–214, *213*
Silk sutures, **172**
Silver-impregnated dressings, **157**
Sinus wounds, **154**
Skin
  biopsies, 267–276
  burrowing ectoparasites, 256–258
  fluid therapy monitoring, 79
  grafts, **154**
  lump removal, 273–276, *273*
  preparation for surgery, 142
  subcutaneous injections *see* Subcutaneous injections
  sutures, 169–170, *171*, **172**
  wound classifications, **154**
Skin twitches, horses, 340
Skull radiography, 209–211, *209*, *210*
Slug bait poisoning, **184**
Smear preparation
  bacterial, 252–253
  blood, 248, *248*
  cytology, 238
  faecal, 242
  mites, 258
  ringworm, 255
Snakes, 323–325, 330–332
  patients bitten by, **191**
Soda lime, 114–115
Sodium bicarbonate, **122**
Sodium chloride (NaCl), 66
  dressings, **157**
  see also Saline
Spinal damage, lifting dogs with, 4–5, *5*
  see also Recumbent patients
Spinal radiographs, 214–215, *214*, *215*
  myelography, 221–222, *221*
Splints, **158**, 164–165, 351–352
Spore strips, **130**
Squamous cell carcinoma, **268**
Starch, detection in faeces, 242
Status epilepticus, 57
Steinmann pins, **170**
Sterilization, 128–129
  autoclaves, 128–129, 231–237
  efficacy monitoring, 130, **130**
  equipment care, 231–237
  ethylene oxide, 128, 129
  folding drapes for, 142–145, *143*
  folding surgical gowns for, 136–141, *138*, *139*
  hot-air ovens, 128
  laboratory equipment, 231–237
  laboratory waste, 237
  packing materials for, 130–132, **131**
  radiation, 128, 129
Stethoscopes
  abdominal assessment in horses, 348
  anaesthesia monitoring, **117**
  pulse rate measurement, 28–29, 346
  respiratory rate measurement, 29–30
Stomach injuries, **193**
Struvite crystals, *261*
Stupor, **177**
Subcutaneous fluid therapy, 68–69
Subcutaneous injections
  cats, 19, *19*
  diabetes mellitus, 61, 62
  dogs, 9–10
  ferrets, 312
  horses, 353
  rabbits, 293
  reptiles, 325, 328, 329
  small rodents, **307**
Subcutaneous tumours, **268**, 269–270, 275–276
Sudan 3, 238
  fat detection in faeces, 242
Sump drains, **167**
Supported exercise, 51, *51*, 57
Surgery
  anaesthesia, 99–126
  illness energy requirement, 84
  theatre practice, 127–152
  see also Surgical nursing procedures; Surgical procedures, minor
Surgical biopsies, 267–271
Surgical gloves, **137**, 138, 139–141, *140*
Surgical gowns, 136–141, **137**, *138*, *139*, *140*
Surgical instruments
  care and maintenance, 146–148
  dental, *172*, **174**
  handling and passing, 146
  'palming', 264, *264*
  surgical kits, 147–148
  trolley preparation, 145
  use of, 264–266
Surgical nursing procedures, 153–174
  bandaging, 157–165, **158**
  dentistry, 170–173
  drainage systems, 167–168
  fractures, **158**, 164–165, 168–169, **170**
  sutures, 169–170, *171*, **172**
  wound management, 153–159, 169–170, 176, 190–192
Surgical procedures, minor, 263–286
  abscesses, 266–267
  aural haematomata, 283–284
  catheter placement for fluid therapy, 276–278
  competence, 263–264
  instrument use, 264–266
  legal position, 263–264, 284
  lump removal, 273–276
  nasolacrimal duct flushing, 280–282
  onychectomy, 279–285
  skin biopsy techniques, 267–276
  suturing pinna wounds, 282–283
  tail tip removal, 284–285
  wound closure, 271–273
Surgical scrub, 134–135, *135*
Suturing kits, *148*
Suturing techniques/materials, 169–170, *171*, **172**, 272, 282–283
Swabs
  skin preparation, 142
  swabbing during surgery, 146
Syrian hamster *see* Hamster (Syrian/Golden)
Syringe pumps, 124, *124*
Syringes
  fine-needle aspirates, 270–271, *270*
  insulin, 61
  intraperitoneal fluid therapy, 70
  oral feed/medication administration, 86
    cats, 17
    dogs, 8
    ferrets, 312
    fluid therapy, 68
    food selection, 85
    horses, 352, *353*
    rabbits, 291–293
    small rodents, 305
  subcutaneous fluid therapy, 69

T

Tablet administration
  cats, 16–23, *16*
  dogs, 7–14, *7*
Tachycardia, **119**, **122**
Tachypnoea, **119**
Taenia spp. eggs/oocysts, *240*
Tail bandages, **158**, 164, *165*
Tail tip removal, 284–285, *285*
Tape muzzles, 2–5, *2*
Tear duct flushing, 280–282, *281*
Tear production
  measuring, 37–38, *38*
  normal volume, **26**
Teeth
  dental instruments, **174**

Trachea
  injuries to,
  intubation s
  obstruction,
  temporary c
Tracheostomie
Transfusions, b
Trauma, illness
Trichodectes cc
Trichoepithelio
Trichophyton s
Trichuris spp. e
Trocars, 50
Trombicula aut
Tube feeding
  food selectio
  gastrostomy,
  maintenance
  nasogastric, 8
  naso-oesopha
  pharyngostom
Tumours, **154**
  biopsy techni
  common skin
  emergency fir
  lump removal
Turtles, 325–328
Twitches, horses,
Tympanic bullae

U

Ulcers, **154**
  decubitus, 57
Ultrasonic scalers
Ultrasound, diagr
Uncinaria spp. eg
Unconsciousness
Uraemia, **193**
Urate crystals, 26
Urethral obstruct
Urethrography, 2
Urinary catheters,
  anaesthetic em
Urine
  anaesthesia mc
  blood in, 58
  cardiac failure
  catheters *see* U
  colour, 259
  cystocentesis, 4
  diabetes insipid
  diabetes mellitu
  dipstick tests, 2
  examination, 25
  fluid therapy mc
  horses, 344